New York Times Best-Selling Authors
Henry Winkler & Lin Oliver

HANK

Here's

Bookmarks Are People Too!

ILLUSTRATED BY SCOTT GARRETT

Grosset & Dunlap

An Imprint of Penguin Group (USA) LLC

To all the teachers who understand the child
who learns differently. To Stacey always—HW

For Leo Pasquale Confalone,
darling SCBWI poster boy!—LO

For my beautiful boys, Texas & Tennessee—SG

GROSSET & DUNLAP
Published by the Penguin Group
Penguin Group (USA) LLC, 375 Hudson Street, New York, New York 10014, USA

USA | Canada | UK | Ireland | Australia | New Zealand | India | South Africa | China

penguin.com
A Penguin Random House Company

Text copyright © 2014 by Henry Winkler and Lin Oliver Productions, Inc.
Illustrations copyright © 2014 by Scott Garrett. All rights reserved.
Published by Grosset & Dunlap, a division of Penguin Young Readers
Group, 345 Hudson Street, New York, New York, 10014.
GROSSET & DUNLAP is a trademark of Penguin
Group (USA) LLC. Printed in the USA.

Typeset in Dyslexie Font B.V.
Dyslexie Font B.V. was designed by Christian Boer.

Library of Congress Cataloging-in-Publication Data is available.

ISBN 978-0-448-47997-2 (pbk)   10 9 8 7 6 5 4 3 2 1
ISBN 978-0-448-48239-2 (hc)   10 9 8 7 6 5 4 3 2 1

The books in the Here's Hank series are designed using the font Dyslexie. A Dutch graphic designer and dyslexic, Christian Boer, developed the font specifically for dyslexic readers. It's designed to make letters more distinct from one another and to keep them tied down, so to speak, so that the reader is less likely to flip them in their minds. The letters in the font are also spaced wide apart to make reading them easier.

Dyslexie has characteristics that make it easier for people with dyslexia to distinguish (and not jumble, invert, or flip) individual letters, such as: heavier bottoms (b, d), larger than normal openings (c, e), and longer ascenders and descenders (f, h, p).

This fun-looking font will help all kids—not just those who are dyslexic—read faster, more easily, and with fewer errors. If you want to know more about the Dyslexie font please visit the site www.dyslexiefont.com.

CHAPTER 1

"Hank Zipzer! Please stop talking!" Ms. Flowers said to me. "Good citizens don't talk when the teacher is talking."

"But I didn't say anything, Ms. Flowers."

"Hank, I saw your lips moving with my own two eyes."

"But no sound came out, Ms. Flowers. So, technically, I wasn't talking."

"Then what exactly were you doing?"

"I was sending a signal."

The other kids in the class laughed, which made me feel great. I wasn't trying to be funny. But it's always nice to get a laugh.

My grandfather Papa Pete always says laughter is good, but not as good as a pickle. We're both big pickle fans.

"And to whom was this so-called signal being sent?" Ms. Flowers asked.

"To me!" Frankie Townsend called out.

Frankie and I have been best friends since we were babies. We have a whole system of signals.

"We can talk without saying a word," I told Ms. Flowers.

"Oh, really?" she said. "That's very unusual."

"There was this one time in the Museum of Natural History," Frankie went on. "It was amazing. Hank and I both decided to roar right in the T. rex's face— at the very same moment."

"It was awesome," I added. "Until the guard told us there was no roaring allowed in the museum."

I laughed, and everyone joined in. Ms. Flowers chuckled, too. She's really nice about laughing. Everyone at PS 87 wants her for second grade because she's in a good mood almost all the time. She even gave me a NICE TRY when I only got two out of ten right on my spelling test last week.

"Well, Hank, since you're so expert at roaring and signaling," she said to me, "you're going to love our next class project."

"I can hardly wait to hear what it is. I'm sitting on the edge of my seat."

"I can hardly wait for you to fall off!" Nick McKelty shouted from the desk behind me.

Nick McKelty, better known as Nick the Tick, never has a nice word to say about anyone.

But he gets away with it because he's about twelve feet tall— in every direction.

"That's enough, Nick," Ms. Flowers snapped, putting her hands on her hips. But McKelty didn't seem to care that she was angry. He just went back to what he always does— rolling spitballs to launch at the little kids during recess.

"Next week is Children's Reading Week," Ms. Flowers went on. "We will be celebrating by putting on a play. I wrote it myself. It's called *A Night at the Library*."

Katie Sperling put up her hand and waved it around.

"Can I be the star?" she asked. "My daddy always tells me I am one, anyway."

"Everyone will have a part," Ms. Flowers said.

"Even me?" Luke Whitman asked, with his finger up his nose.

"Yes, even you, Luke."

I wondered if there was a part in the play for a champion nose-picker.

Luke Whitman would get that
for sure!

"I think we all know who's
going to be the star!" McKelty
shouted out. "The one with the
most talent. And that would be
me."

Then, for no reason at all,
he stood up and bowed, and let
out one of his snorty laughs. No
one else joined in.

"I'm now going to pass out
the script," Ms. Flowers said,
motioning for McKelty to sit
down. "Read the play over the
weekend and decide on which
part you'd like."

I felt worried. Really worried.
Regular second-grade reading is

hard for me. Reading a whole script would be nearly impossible.

Frankie saw my face and sent me our "don't worry" signal. I relaxed right away, because I knew he would help me. Frankie is an excellent reader. Over winter break, he read a two-hundred-page book that didn't even have pictures.

"We will hold auditions on Monday," Ms. Flowers told us. "That's when you can each try out for the part you want."

Even though I knew Frankie would help me, I was starting to get very nervous.

"You'll have to study your lines and be very prepared,"

Ms. Flowers continued. "Does anyone have any questions?"

As usual, I had *many* questions. Also as usual, I was too embarrassed to ask them. So I did what I usually did— I made a list in my head.

CHAPTER 2

Questions I Have about the Play
(That I'm Too Afraid To Ask)
BY HANK ZIPZER

1. Will I be any good at this?
2. I mean, will I *really* be any good at this?
3. What if I'm not good at this?
4. Can you throw up during an audition and still get the part?
5. And the big question: Will I be any good at this? Oh, I already said that.

CHAPTER 3

After school that day, Papa Pete picked up Frankie and me. Frankie's mom is a yoga instructor, and she teaches every Friday afternoon. She is so good at yoga that she can lift her foot off the floor and squeeze her nose with her toes like they're a swimmer's clip.

While Frankie's mom's teaching, Papa Pete takes Frankie and me to the Crunchy Pickle. That's the deli on 77th Street and Broadway

that Papa Pete used to own.
Now my mom is taking it over
and trying to turn it into
a healthy sandwich shop.

That is very bad news for
salami.

As we walked toward the
Crunchy Pickle, Frankie and I
couldn't stop talking about
the play. Actually, I did all the
talking, and Frankie did all
the listening.

"I was in a play once when
I was your age," Papa Pete said
when I finally took a breath.

"Were you the star?" I asked
him.

"Not exactly. I played a tube

of toothpaste, but it was a very important tube. Harold Dunski was the star. He was lucky enough to get the part of Mr. Toothbrush."

"What's so lucky about that?" I asked.

"Are you kidding, Hankie?" Papa Pete said. "Harold got to sing the big opening number. It was called 'Don't Forget to Flush and Brush.' The girls went crazy. In fact, years later he married the girl who played the sink."

"No offense, Papa Pete," Frankie said, "but this is kind of a disgusting story."

"Well, I'm just pointing out that being in a play is a lot of fun, but it's also a lot of work. You have rehearsals to go to, lines to memorize . . ."

"That's the part that scares me the most," I said. "I'm pretty bad at memorizing. I can't even remember how to spell *neighbor*."

"Don't be so hard on yourself, Hankie," Papa Pete said. "You're clever. You'll figure it out."

I wasn't so sure he was right about that.

We had reached the entrance to the Crunchy Pickle. Papa Pete pulled open the glass door. Frankie and I dashed to the counter that held the black-and-white cookies. They've been our favorite ever since I can remember. Just before we grabbed two, my mom came out from the back room.

"Whoa there, mister," she said. "No cookies until you've had a healthy snack. I have some fresh soylami right here."

My mom is trying to bring luncheon meats into the twenty-first century. She makes everything out of soy. Soylami, which tastes nothing like salami. Soystrami, which makes your tongue want to go home without eating. And the worst is soyloney, which doesn't

even *look* like baloney. In fact,
it's yellow.

"Mom!" I protested. "Frankie
and I have a lot of work to do,
and we need real brain food."

"Look at your sister," she
answered. "See how nicely
she's sitting in that front booth
enjoying her soy-meat platter?"

My sister, Emily, who is in

the first grade, does everything perfectly. It's just like her to enjoy fake meat. She also likes doing her homework, reading about lizards, clipping her toenails, and getting all As. She is so annoying.

"Why don't you boys find a seat," Papa Pete said. "I'll make you a real sandwich, with some pickles on the side."

Papa Pete is just the best. He saves the day, every day.

Frankie and I slid into a

booth far away from Emily. We reached into our backpacks and each pulled out a copy of the play. As soon as I turned to the first page, my brain froze like a Popsicle.

"I can't read this," I said to Frankie. "It's too many words."

"Yes you can, Hank. Let's go very slowly."

Frankie read the summary of the story.

"It's about a boy named Barry who falls asleep in the library," he explained. "While he's asleep, the books come alive and jump off the shelves."

"Wow, that sounds great. Does it say what kinds of books?"

Frankie nodded. "The books are all the characters the class is going to play. Look, there's a book on volcanoes."

"That'd be great for Luke Whitman," I said. "His nose is always full of lava." We cracked up, and Frankie went on.

"Let's see. There's a biography of Martin Luther King Jr. And a mystery story called *The Secret of Big Bear Lake.* Here's a scary one called *My Babysitter Is a Zombie.* And look at this weird one— *The History of Shoes Up to the Flip-Flop.* You interested in that part?"

"No," I said, shaking my head. "I can't stand anything between my toes."

"Oh, this book is cool," Frankie said, pointing to some words on the page. "It's a superhero comic book called *Aqua Fly.* It's about a fly that lives in an underwater cave."

"That's perfect for me!"
I said. "I'm going for that part.
What about you, Frankie?"

"I think I'd be good at
playing Barry. I like to read in
the library. And I'm really good
at falling asleep."

"Great, then we both know
what we want," I said. "Let's
get to work."

I flipped through my script.
All the words started to swim
on the pages. I was hoping
that Aqua Fly didn't have too
many words to say. Maybe he
would just fly and buzz. I could
buzz for thirty-seven minutes
straight if I had to.

Unfortunately, Aqua Fly was

pretty talkative. As I tried to read all his lines, I could feel my brain start to swirl. After a few more pages, it felt like all I had in my head was soggy oatmeal.

"Here are your sandwiches, boys," Papa Pete said, sliding our plates onto the table next to the scripts.

Boy, oh, boy. I was never so glad to see a turkey sandwich and a pickle. They didn't have to read me, and I didn't have to read them. All I had to do was eat. And I am a champion eater.

CHAPTER 4

Frankie and I stayed at the Crunchy Pickle for over an hour, eating our sandwiches and working on our lines.

As more customers came in, my mom said she needed the booth. So I kissed her good-bye, and Papa Pete took Frankie and me and, I'm sorry to say, Emily back to our apartment building.

Frankie lives on the fourth floor, and my family lives on the tenth. He and I have a special clubhouse in the basement, right next to the laundry room. It's actually a storage room that we made into our clubhouse. We hang out there because it's really fun. Also, the air smells like soap suds, which is very refreshing for my nose.

When we got home, we tried to continue our work on my dining-room table. My dad even moved his computer down to one end to make room for us. Also he put on shoes so we didn't have to look at his toenails.

As Frankie and I started

going over the lines, my dad
looked up from his computer
screen.

"That doesn't sound like schoolwork to me," he said.

"We're getting ready to audition for our class play," Frankie explained.

"Hank, you should be working on your writing and arithmetic skills," my dad said. "No one ever did well on a test by being in a play."

"This play is going to be really fun, Dad," I said. "And very educational, too."

"Oh, really?" my dad snapped. "Well then, how much is forty minus eighteen?"

I looked in every corner of my mind for the answer. It was nowhere to be found.

My brain can hear numbers, but it has no idea what to do with them. I mean, addition is hard. But subtraction is out of the question.

"I'll get back to you with the answer, Dad," I said. "In about five years."

"Trust me, Hank, it won't be that long," he said. "After dinner, I'm getting out the flash cards. It's going to be an all-subtraction evening."

What a horrible thought. Then, even more horribly, Emily

decided to take her baby pet
iguana, Katherine, on a walk
around the apartment. Every
time they passed, Katherine
shot her tongue out and tried
to touch my knuckles. One time
she actually did. And let me
tell you, iguana tongue is very
sticky and rough.

"Okay," I announced. "That does it for me. It's clubhouse time."

"You don't have to leave," Emily said. "Katherine enjoys the company."

"Oh, really? Then why is she hissing at us like a fire-breathing dragon?" Frankie asked.

"That's her way of saying *give me a hug*."

"Well, tell her my body is a hug-free zone," I answered. "Especially when it comes to lizards."

"She's an *iguana*, Hank."

"Whatever she is, she's ugly."

With that, a superloud hiss flew out of Katherine's throat.

Frankie and I dashed out of the apartment and into the elevator. Forty-two seconds later, we were in our clubhouse in the basement.

But there was already someone there!

As we rushed in, we saw a woman in a flowered dress standing on a ladder. Holding the ladder steady was a girl about our age. *A girl in our clubhouse? No, that's not in the rulebook.*

"Hi," the girl said, turning to us. "I'm Ashley Wong. I just moved into the building, and I'm starting second grade tomorrow at PS Eighty-Seven."

"We're second-graders, too," Frankie said.

"Look at that! We've almost got a whole class in here," I added.

Ashley cracked up at that. "You're funny," she said.

"Hank's a riot," Frankie said. "He keeps everyone laughing. We call it the Zipzer attitude."

"Are you looking for something, Mrs. Wong?" I asked the woman in the flowered dress who I guessed was Ashley's mother. "Frankie and I know everything in here."

"Mrs. Park keeps her dog's raincoats in the box in the corner," Frankie said.

"And Mrs. Fink keeps her gently used bathrobes in that big plastic container," I added. "Watch out if you go in there, though. You don't want to be digging around and suddenly find a set of her false teeth."

Ashley covered her mouth to hold in a laugh.

"We were putting away some boxes," Mrs. Wong said, climbing down from the ladder. "Our family just moved into an apartment on the seventh floor and there isn't much closet space. We're finished now."

"Mom, can I stay down here with these guys?" Ashley asked.

"Of course, honey, if it's all

right with them. Just be back by dinnertime. Your grandmother is making wonton soup."

"So, what do you want to do?" Ashley asked us.

Frankie and I just stood there with our mouths hanging open. This was *our* clubhouse. No girls allowed.

"Uh, actually, we have a lot of work to do down here," I said, trying to be polite. "We have to memorize lines for Ms. Flowers's class play. Auditions are on Monday."

"Ms. Flowers!" Ashley exclaimed. "She's going to be my teacher, too. If I learn the play now, think what a great head start I'll have. This is just *so* perfect!"

Without waiting to be asked, she flopped down on the old flowered couch. The one that Frankie and I always sit on.

"You guys have the play?" she asked as her mom left. Then she noticed it lying on one of the cardboard boxes. She picked it up and starting flipping through the pages.

"Which part do you want, Hank?"

"Aqua Fly," I muttered. "I'm an excellent buzzer."

Ashley pushed her purple glasses back on her nose and laughed.

"You are such a crack-up," she said, holding up her hand for a high five.

"Thanks," I said. I have to admit, I was beginning to like Ashley, even if she was a girl.

"Check it out, guys," Ashley said, continuing to turn the pages. Unlike me, she seemed to be able to read at lightning speed. "This part is totally me— the zombie from *My Babysitter Is a Zombie*. I have a great zombie walk."

She jumped to her feet and held her arms out in front of

her body. Then she staggered around the clubhouse, bumping into dusty boxes, old lamps, and piles of clothes. Each time she hit something, she let out a long moan. All of a sudden, she turned to Frankie and me and pulled down on her eyes so you could see the icky red part inside.

"Zombie attack!" she screeched, lunging forward until she fell on the couch in a heap, laughing her head off. Frankie and I held our sides and howled, too.

And just like that, Ashley Wong became one of us.

CHAPTER 5

The three of us spent all weekend working on the play. Sometimes we were each in our own apartments. Sometimes we met in the clubhouse.

Of course, we took breaks. On Saturday, we went to Riverside Park for a snowball fight. Unfortunately, we ran into Nick the Tick McKelty there. When Frankie and I introduced him to Ashley, the first thing he did was make fun of her purple glasses.

Right away, McKelty found out that wasn't such a great idea when she whacked him on the nose with a snowball. It turns out Ashley Wong has the arm of a shortstop.

"Hey!" McKelty yelled, a clump of snow sliding down into his mouth. "Nobody messes with me."

"I just did," Ashley said. "You can make fun of my glasses all you want. But they helped me see well enough to hit you smack in the nose."

That shut him up. But Ashley wasn't finished.

"And as you can see," she added, "there is plenty more snow left."

McKelty had no comeback to that. He just ran off whimpering like a hurt puppy.

On Monday morning, my mom walked Frankie, Emily, and me to school. As we left the apartment, we ran into Ashley and her mom, who were on their way to school, too.

"Hello, I'm Dr. Wong,"
Ashley's mother said, extending
her hand to my mom.

"So nice to meet you,"
my mom answered. "I'm Randi
Zipzer. Silly me. When I saw

Dr. Wong written on your mailbox, I thought it was your husband."

"He *is* Dr. Wong. And so am I."

"So your parents are Dr. Wong and Dr. Wong?" Emily asked.

"Exactly," Ashley said. "And they want me to be a doctor when I grow up, too. Then we'll be Dr. Wong, Dr. Wong, and Dr. Wong. But I think that's just wrong."

Frankie and I cracked up.

As we all headed up 78th Street toward Amsterdam Avenue, Ashley asked Frankie if he was ready for the audition.

"Sure," he said. "I have my script right here in my backpack with my lines highlighted in yellow."

Script! Did he say script? Oh no. Where was *my* script? Suddenly, I couldn't remember where I'd put it. Was it in my backpack? Or did I leave it on the breakfast table next to the cereal box? I closed my eyes and tried to remember. As usual, my brain came up blank.

"Hold it, everyone," I said. "Stop right where you are."

I spun around so my back was facing Frankie.

"Unzip my backpack," I asked him. "And please tell me my script is in there."

I could feel Frankie tugging on the zipper. Then I could feel his hand rummaging around inside.

"Is it there?" I asked.

"Give me a minute, Hankster. I'm still digging my way through the cookie crumbs and bubble-gum wrappers. Don't you ever clean this thing out?"

"This is not the time to talk about neatness, Frankie."

"But it is the time to tell you that there is no script in here."

"You forgot it?" Emily, the Perfect One, said. "Honestly, Hank, we should put a Post-it note on your forehead."

"I have to go back and get it," I said.

"There isn't time, Hank," my mom said, checking her watch.

"Yeah," Emily piped up. "Just because the only thing you remember to pack are cookie crumbs, doesn't mean I have to be late for school."

"Emily, did anyone ever tell you your braids are too tight?" I snapped.

"Don't worry about it, dude," Frankie said before Emily could answer. "You can use my script when it's your turn to audition."

"But mine was all highlighted and everything."

"I'll highlight your lines in blue when we get to school," Frankie told me. "I'll be yellow, you'll be blue."

"Hey, together you'll make green," Ashley said.

As we started walking toward school, I could feel my mother's hand on my shoulder. I hoped she wasn't going to lecture me. I was already very upset about forgetting my script. And I was nervous about the audition, too. The last thing I needed was a lecture.

"I know this is the last thing you need . . . ," my mom began.

Oh no, here it comes.

"But we have to talk about you being better organized, Hank," she continued. "We've gone over this many times."

"I try, Mom. I really do. But every time I think I'm organized, it turns out that I'm not. I don't get it."

"You have to focus," she said. "Your mind is running all over the place."

She was right. I needed to focus. And at that moment, the

thing I needed to concentrate
on was the audition. I made
my brain focus on Aqua Fly.
I forced it to buzz. I imagined
that I was a superhero.
I thought superhero thoughts.

I was so focused I didn't see the patch of ice on the sidewalk in front of me. I stepped on it and slid about four feet before falling on my butt. One leg headed north, and the other one headed south. My hat flew off and landed in a puddle.

I just sat on the ground, feeling the icy water soaking into the seat of my pants. And let me tell you this: I never felt less like a superhero in my whole life.

CHAPTER 6

I spent morning recess standing as close as I could to the heater in Principal Love's office. I wasn't in any trouble. It's just that he happens to have the most powerful heater in my school. I didn't care where I was. I just wanted to unfreeze my underpants from my butt. Trust me, it's no fun having icicles in your tighty-whities.

When the bell rang,
I checked my bottom. It was
warm and mostly dry. As I
hurried for the door, Principal
Love tapped me on the
shoulder.

"Your hat, Hank," he said,
handing me my damp blue knit
cap. "Is there anything you
don't forget?"

"I never forget my birthday,
Principal Love."

"Hank, always remember
these words: Being forgetful
puts you on the road to
nowhere."

That didn't make any sense.

"Principal Love, can I ask
you a question? How can there

be a road to nowhere? I mean, isn't nowhere *nowhere*?"

"You'll understand what I'm talking about when you're my age," he said. He licked two fingers and slicked down the single strand of hair on his bald head.

Holy cow. I hope when I'm his age, I have more hair.

I got to class just as the bell rang. Ms. Flowers had

already listed everybody's name on the blackboard. Next to each name was a blank space where she would write what part each person was chosen to play.

"Okay, class," Ms. Flowers began. "I know you're all nervous. But there's no need to be. Just do the best you can. Let's start with our newest student, Ashley Wong. She was lucky enough to be able to go over the script this weekend with some new friends she made."

Ashley smiled at Frankie and me.

"Everyone say, 'Welcome, Ashley,'" Ms. Flowers continued.

We did. Then Ashley walked up to the front of the class, dragging a leg zombie-style behind her. She went right into her babysitter zombie performance.

"Listen, kids," she moaned to three imaginary children. "Don't worry about my eyeball dropping to the ground. I'll pick it up later."

Everyone laughed and applauded. Ashley took a bow and sat down.

"Excellent," Ms. Flowers said. "I see we have a little actress among us. What a great way to start off our auditions."

Luke Whitman went next. He set a new low on the disgusting scale when he made a volcano erupt through his nose. Halfway through, Ms. Flowers had to send him to the nurse's office for emergency nose repair.

Katie Sperling did a great
job playing a pop-up book.
Every time she turned a page,
she jumped so high her pigtails
stood straight up.

But the best of everyone
was Frankie playing the part of
Barry. He had memorized every
line, and there were a lot of
them. When he pretended to
fall asleep, it was so real
you actually thought he was
dreaming. I clapped like crazy
when he was done. Everyone
joined in. We all knew there
was no one else that could
play Barry.

Then it was my turn.

"Hank, what part have

you chosen to audition for?"
Ms. Flowers asked.

"Aqua Fly," I answered.

My heart was thumping as I walked to the front of the class, holding Frankie's script. I passed Ashley's desk.

"You're going to be great," she whispered.

It seemed to take forever to reach the front of the room. When I got there, Ms. Flowers had to remind me to turn and face the class. I took a deep breath and looked down at the script. All I saw was a sea of blue highlights. Those were the very words I had gone over all weekend long. And I didn't recognize one of them.

"Hank, you can start any
time you're ready," I heard
Ms. Flowers say.

I couldn't read. All I could
manage to do was buzz. It
seemed like I buzzed for twenty
minutes. Finally, Ms. Flowers
interrupted my buzz fest.

"Are you going to say any of the lines?" she asked.

"I am saying the lines," I answered. "I'm just doing it in fly language."

"Interesting," she said. "But I really do need to hear what's written in the script."

I looked at the pages again. Zero. Zippo. Nothing doing.

I had no choice but to buzz to my seat and sit down. The audition was a total flop. My only hope of getting the part was if no one else volunteered.

"Is there anyone else who wants to try out for Aqua Fly?" Ms. Flowers asked.

No one answered. That was

just what I was hoping for. The part was mine. *Aqua Fly, here I come.*

And then, one single hand popped into the air.

It belonged to Nick McKelty. I had no choice but to make another list in my head.

CHAPTER 7

Five Things I Hope Will Happen to Nick Mckelty During His Audition
BY HANK ZIPZER

1. His teeth will turn green and start to glow.

2. An alien spaceship will come through the ceiling and take him to their planet until summer.

3. He'll open his mouth to talk and only hiccupy burps will come out.

4. He will actually turn into a fly and buzz right out the window.

5. Oops! I only have time for four. Mckelty is about to start.

CHAPTER 8

Unfortunately for me, none of the things on my list happened. What did happen was that McKelty got the part of Aqua Fly. If you ask me, it wasn't because he was so great. It was because, unlike me, he could read the words on the page.

Ms. Flowers tried to be nice about it. When everyone was going to lunch, she called me up to her desk.

"I know you tried really hard, Hank," she said. "And for your effort, I have created a special part just for you. One that matches your talents."

That made me feel much better. But what part could that be? Maybe there was going to be a big clock on the library wall, and I would be the bird that popped out every hour and went *cuckoo*. Everyone knows I'm good at sounds.

Or maybe I could be the library cart that gets to roll up and down the aisles. I could attach my bicycle horn and toot it to warn everyone to clear the way for me. That sounded like a lot of fun.

"What is my part, Ms. Flowers?"

"Well, Hank, you are going to be a bookmark."

"I *am*? What does a bookmark get to do?"

"First of all, you have to be very quiet. And of course, your most important job will be to hold everyone's places in their books."

"That doesn't sound fun."

"But here's the best part.

You'll get to wear the tallest costume of anyone, with two little holes cut out for your eyes. And a red fringe on the bottom to cover your shoes."

Okay, I could deal with that. The costume part sounded good. I left the classroom feeling pretty happy about my new role . . . until I walked into the lunch room. The first person I saw was McKelty, who was busy shoving tuna casserole into his face right off his tray. He wasn't even using a fork.

"Hey, loser," he said, spraying little bits of fish into

the air. "Too bad I beat you out
for the good part."

"That's okay," I said to him.
"I'm going to be a bookmark."

"Ha-ha-ha." He snorted.
"Don't you get it? A bookmark
doesn't do anything. It
just stands there being all
bookmark-y."

"Oh yeah?" I answered back.
"Ms. Flowers said it was a
really special part."

"You'll believe anything, Zipperbrain!" Then he added, "See you after lunch in rehearsal. Oh wait, you don't have to be there. You don't have any lines."

"I'll be there," I snapped. "I'm part of the play, too."

"Oh, really. Then how come your part isn't even in the script?"

That was a good question. I hadn't thought of that before. Then I realized what had happened. Ms. Flowers had made up that part just for me because I can't read very well.

Suddenly, the smell of

tuna casserole coming out of McKelty's mouth made me feel sick to my stomach. I ran out into the hall and leaned against the wall, trying so hard not to cry. Before I knew it, Frankie and Ashley had left the cafeteria and were by my side.

"Don't listen to that big bully," Ashley said. "Bookmarks are very important. I use one every day."

"But it's just a tiny part," I protested.

"Listen, Hankster," Frankie said. "No matter what the part is, you're going to be great."

"Yeah," Ashley chimed in.

"Just wait until rehearsal. You never know what magic is going to come spilling out of that funny head of yours."

Suddenly I was starving, which was a sure sign that I was feeling better. Friends can do that for you.

"Okay," I said, heading back into the cafeteria with Frankie and Ashley by my side. "I'm going to be the best bookmark that ever held a place in a book. Look out, world, here comes Hank."

Oh, and by the way, about the tuna casserole: If you ever see even a glop of it on your plate, change plates. I didn't, and my tongue is still not talking to me.

CHAPTER 9

After lunch, we went back to class. Ms. Flowers had moved all the desks into a wide semicircle, so we had the entire center of the room to rehearse our play.

"Let's have all people playing books stand on the left," she said, "and everyone else on the right."

I followed her directions.

"No, Hank," Ms. Flowers said. "You're supposed to be on the right."

"I know," I answered.
"That's where I am."

"Hank, you are on the left side," she explained. "Do you know which way is left and which is right?"

"I always guess, and every now and then I'm right."

"Well, not this time, Zipperfang," McKelty said with a snort. "Only a birdbrain doesn't know right from left."

"You better not ruffle the feathers of this bird, McKelty!" I shot back.

Everyone laughed, and I felt pretty good about that. The score: Hank Zipzer, one. Nick McKelty, zero.

Ms. Flowers led me to my place. Then Frankie sat down at a table she had put in the center of the circle.

"You may begin reading your lines," she said to him. "Remember that you are alone in the library, and it's late at night."

Frankie yawned and stretched.

"'The library is so dark and quiet when everyone is gone,'" he read. "'It feels like a magical place where anything could happen.'"

He put his head down on the table and pretended to fall asleep.

"'I wonder if I'll dream about books,'" he muttered, just before he closed his eyes.

"Excellent," Ms. Flowers said. "Remember to say your lines loud enough so everyone can hear you. And now, all the children who are playing books start to come alive. Think about the title of your book, and then come up with the way you would move."

Instantly, Ashley went into her zombie walk. McKelty flapped his arms and started to buzz like Aqua Fly. Luke threw his arms over his head and pretended he was an erupting volcano. I was standing next to

Luke, and let me tell you, this volcano never showered. When his arms went over his head, his armpits smelled like rotten bananas.

My nose started to twitch. The hairs inside felt like they were curling up into little hair balls. Without even thinking, I moved away from him and found myself in the middle of the circle.

"Hank," Ms. Flowers said. "You're playing a bookmark. You're supposed to be *in* the books, not in front of them."

"But I'm a bookmark with a lot of personality," I said.

Everyone laughed again, so I started to think about what a bookmark with a lot of personality would do. He wouldn't just sit between the pages of a book. Maybe he would wiggle his way to another page. You know, like a worm crawling around on the ground.

As soon as that thought popped into my brain, I dropped to the floor. My body was off and wiggling across the stage area.

"What are you doing, Hank?" Ms. Flowers said with a smile. I guess she had never seen a bookmark flopping across her classroom before.

"I am looking for my place in the best book," I said.

"Well then, wiggle on over to me," Ashley said. "Zombies are always fun to read about."

I twisted and squirmed and rolled all the way over to Ashley. Everybody in class was cracking up. Even Ms. Flowers couldn't stop herself from laughing.

"You're not going to put that stupid wiggling junk in the play, are you?" McKelty grumbled. His face was as red as a radish.

"Are you kidding?" Frankie said to him. "Hank is being really funny."

"But he's not supposed to be funny," McKelty answered. "Besides, the parents are here to see *me* in the play. *I'm* the star."

There he was, being Nick McKelty again. He never tells the truth. It's always the truth times one hundred. Frankie and I call that the McKelty factor. Ashley didn't know about the McKelty factor. But when she heard it in action, she went nuts.

"You are so not the star of the play," she said to him. "Every one of us is important. And remember, you're a fly. Everyone wants to swat you."

We all cracked up at that. Boy, oh, boy, did that ever make McKelty mad. He frowned so hard his lips almost dropped to the floor.

"Okay, everyone,"
Ms. Flowers said, trying to
settle us all down. "We have
a lot of work to do. The play
is only two days away."

"So can I keep the wiggle
in?" I asked her.

"Only if you keep it very
short," she said. "Remember,
a little wiggle goes a long
way."

We went on with the
rehearsal, but McKelty kept
giving me angry looks. Once,
when I was standing next
to him, he leaned over and
whispered in my ear.

"You better not try to steal

the show again, Zippernose,"
he said, snarling at me through
his slimy green teeth. It looked
like there was a bunch of
lettuce growing in there.

"What are you going to

do about it?" I snarled back.

"Let's just say, you'll be sorry."

I gulped hard. As much as I don't like to admit it, that Nick McKelty can be very scary.

CHAPTER 10

All the next day, we rehearsed very hard. The best part about it was that we got to skip math and spelling. Any day I can skip math is a good day for my brain. And not having to take a spelling test is like a mini vacation. By the end of school, everyone seemed ready.

Since I didn't have any lines, my rehearsal time was shorter than everyone else's. So

Ms. Flowers had me work on my bookmark costume. I stapled lots of sheets of construction paper together, and then cut some fringe at the top and the bottom. To make it look really cool, I took a black crayon and wrote the word BOKMARK right down the middle.

"Hey, Zip," Frankie whispered to me on one of his breaks. "Hand me that black crayon."

"How come?"

"You left out one of the *O*s in *book*," he said. "It has two *O*s."

I handed him the crayon, and he added a very skinny *O* to make it look like it had always been there.

I'm so lucky to have a friend like Frankie. He always saves me from being really embarrassed.

The next day was the big performance. All our moms and dads were coming to see us.

We were so excited. Everyone got there early. We helped Ms. Flowers arrange the chairs for the parents around the edge of the classroom. Lots of us brought snacks for the treat table. Frankie's mom made her famous brownies without walnuts, in case any kids were allergic to nuts. Katie Sperling brought rice-crispy treats that she decorated with M&M's. My mom, of course, had to be different. She sent in a deli tray with nothing on it that even looked like food. Well, there was one thing that could have been tuna fish, but nobody was willing to taste it and find out for sure.

Ms. Flowers had us wait in the hall while the parents filed in and took their seats. Once they were in the room, we put on our costumes. Frankie wore just a sweatshirt and jeans.

Ashley had a zombie wig with fake blood dripping off it. The top of my costume went up over my face, so I had to cut out holes for my eyes and mouth.

Just before the play was about to start, Ms. Flowers came out into the hall to check our costumes and give us a pep talk.

"Is everyone ready?" she asked.

"Everyone but Nick McKelty," Ashley answered. "He went to the bathroom."

"I always pee a lot when I'm nervous, too," Luke Whitman said. "Before my oral report on Thomas Edison, I must have gone to the bathroom twenty times."

"That's something we really don't need to know," Katie Sperling said.

"As soon as Nick returns, I'll introduce you," Ms. Flowers said. "There's no reason to be nervous. You all know your lines.

If you just concentrate and work together, nothing will go wrong."

Just then, Nick McKelty ran down the hall. Well, he was half running and half hopping, trying to tie his Aqua Fly wings back on.

"Are you ready, Nick?" Ms. Flowers asked.

"You should have heard me practicing in the bathroom," he bragged. "I crushed it."

"How do you know?" I said to him. "Did all the sinks applaud?"

"That's so funny I forgot to laugh," he snarled.

"That's enough, boys,"
Ms. Flowers said. "Remember,
keep your mind on the play
and enjoy yourselves."

She went into the classroom.

"Welcome to Children's
Reading Week," we heard Ms.
Flowers say to the parents.
"And now, allow me to present
the Room Four Players, starring
in *A Night at the Library*."

The parents clapped as we
all filed in and took our places.

I looked out and saw a sea
of flashing lights, some from
real cameras and some from
cell phones. My mom and dad
were there, and so was Papa
Pete. It was easy to pick him

out because he was wearing his favorite bright red running suit. It makes him look like a ripe strawberry.

The parents got very quiet, and then Frankie began. And once he fell asleep, the "books" came alive. It was all going great. Katie popped up. Luke erupted. And the parents were laughing their heads off.

Then it was Nick McKelty's turn. He buzzed right by me and introduced himself to the audience, adding buzzing sounds in between the words.

"Say hello . . . *buzz* . . . to Aqua Fly . . . *buzz* . . . the most powerful . . . superhero . . . that ever landed on a tomato . . . *buzz*."

The parents laughed, and McKelty seemed pretty pleased with himself.

Then it was my turn.
I stepped out and dropped
to the floor. I wiggled over to
Ashley, being careful not
to over-wiggle. Ashley flashed
me a smile. When I saw that,
it tickled my brain. Suddenly,
from nowhere, my mouth flew
open and in my best bookmark
voice, out came these words:

"I am here to hold your place
and put a big smile on your
face."

I heard the parents laugh.
A few even clapped. I felt
great. I rose to my feet, being
careful not to trip on my fringe.
I turned to face my family,
so they would get a good

picture of me. As I took a
step, I felt something under
my foot. It was a shoe— a big
shoe— that could only belong
to Nick McKelty. He had stuck
his foot out in front of me, and

since I couldn't look down in my costume, I tripped over it.

"Let me know what the floor looks like," McKelty whispered with a nasty laugh. "I told you what would happen if you tried to steal my show." That was the last thing I heard before I fell.

As I was going down, I knew there was nothing I could do to stop it. I was going to make a fool of myself in front of everyone.

Then it came to me. A line, a really funny line, just popped into my head.

"Oops," I said, as I hit the floor. "I lost my *plaaaaaaaaaaaace*."

The audience laughed, thinking it was part of the play. But I didn't laugh. My purple construction paper ripped right in two, and I thought I might have split my pants. I was too scared to look.

The only thing I saw for sure was McKelty's face, laughing down at me.

"Remember, Zippercreep," he said. "I'm the star. Not you!"

And at that moment, lying there on the floor, I totally believed him.

CHAPTER 11

I was sprawled out on the
floor, my costume destroyed,
my pants probably ripped.

I didn't know what to do.
But Ms. Flowers had told us
that an important rule in plays
is that "the show must go on."
No matter what, you have to
keep the show going.

So I figured that the best
thing for me was to get out of
the middle of the stage so the
play could go on. I pulled myself

along the floor until I reached
Ashley, who held out a hand
and dragged me the rest of
the way.

This made Nick McKelty
even angrier, because the parents
weren't watching him, they were
watching me. And let me say,
this was one time I didn't want
to be the center of attention.

"Carry on, kids," Ms. Flowers
whispered. "You know what
comes next."

Frankie lifted his head off
the desk and pretended to wake
up. He yawned and stretched.

"I had the strangest dream,"
he said. "The books were
alive."

Everyone stood very still, except Nick McKelty.

This was the part of the play where Aqua Fly was supposed to buzz over to Frankie and tell him it was not a dream at all. That books always come alive, as long as we believe in them. Ms. Flowers had told us it was the biggest moment of the play. It was the line she was most proud of writing.

McKelty buzzed over and took his place next to Frankie.

He opened his mouth, but all that came out was a buzzing sound. That would have been okay, but the next thing that came out of his mouth was another buzzing sound. And then another one. And another one.

"Say your lines, Nick," Frankie whispered. "We have to finish the play."

"*Buzz*," Nick said. "*Buzz, buzz, buzz!*"

There was panic in his eyes.

"You can't just buzz," Frankie told him.

"*Buzz*," McKelty answered.

"No, say the words!" Frankie whispered.

"I forgot them," McKelty whispered back. I could see his hands starting to shake with fear. He looked like Katherine, the iguana, the first time she saw Papa Pete's cat, Morris.

I looked around and saw
everyone in the audience waiting
for the big ending. Ms. Flowers
was trying to mouth the words
to McKelty, but he wouldn't
look at her. He just stood
there, buzzing.

Without even thinking about
it, I jumped to my feet and

shuffled my way over to Frankie.
He looked just as surprised
as I was. When I opened my
mouth, I couldn't believe what
came out.

"I am just a lowly bookmark,"
I said. "But one thing I know for
sure: Books always come alive
when we believe in them."

"So this wasn't a dream?"
Frankie said.

"No," I answered. "Not at
all. All the books here are alive
and waiting for you whenever
you want to have a great
adventure."

And without thinking, Frankie
and I threw our arms around
each other.

The parents started to
applaud.

"Thanks for coming," I said
to the parents. "The Room Four
Players have enjoyed putting on
this play for you."

All the kids came forward to
take a bow. Everyone but Nick
McKelty. He was still buzzing.

After the play, we all got

behind the treat table and served our parents lemonade and snacks. Luke Whitman was the only one who ate my mom's so-called deli meats. But that wasn't surprising, since he also enjoys already-chewed gum he finds in his pockets.

"Hankie, my boy," Papa Pete said, as I put a rice-crispy treat on his plate. "You were so great. It looked like you saved the day."

"Yes," my mom chimed in. "We thought you didn't have any lines in the play."

"Well," I said. "That's what was supposed to happen. But

when McKelty froze up, I had to jump in."

"But how did you know the lines?" Papa Pete asked.

"I have a good memory," I said. "I learned everyone's lines by hearing them over and over while we were rehearsing."

"Such a smart boy." Papa Pete beamed.

That made me feel very happy. I always think Emily is the smart one in our family, not me.

I really loved it when all the kids and Ms. Flowers thanked me for saving the play. The only one who didn't congratulate me was— you guessed it— Nick McKelty.

"I could have done those lines better than you," he said, shoving his third brownie in his mouth. "Yeah? Well, why didn't you?"

"I wasn't in the mood."

As for me, I was in a really good mood. Even Nick McKelty couldn't make me feel bad. I was on top of the world. I felt great. So great that I just had to make a list.

CHAPTER 12

Three Things

That Make You Feel Great

by Hank Zipzer

Your friends!

Your family!

Yourself!